llama
llama
Anna Dewdney

daddy's day

Based on the bestselling children's
book series by Anna Dewdney

PENGUIN YOUNG READERS LICENSES
An Imprint of Penguin Random House LLC, New York

Penguin supports copyright. Copyright fuels creativity, encourages diverse voices, promotes free speech, and creates a vibrant culture. Thank you for buying an authorized edition of this book and for complying with copyright laws by not reproducing, scanning, or distributing any part of it in any form without permission. You are supporting writers and allowing Penguin to continue to publish books for every reader.

Copyright © Anna E. Dewdney Literary Trust. Copyright © 2021 Genius Brands International, Inc. Published by Penguin Young Readers Licenses, an imprint of Penguin Random House LLC, New York. Manufactured in China.

Visit us online at www.penguinrandomhouse.com.

ISBN 9780593224717   10 9 8 7 6 5 4 3 2 1

Nelly Gnu and Daddy Gnu are hanging out in their front yard.

Nelly Gnu practices tricks on her skateboard.

"This one is called an ollie!" Nelly Gnu says. "Do you want to try?"

"I suppose my chores can wait," Daddy Gnu responds.

He puts on his helmet and grabs the skateboard.

"Whoa!" says Daddy Gnu.
He loses his balance
right away.

"You can practice with my
skateboard anytime," says
Nelly Gnu.
"Thanks," Daddy Gnu replies.
"Maybe one day, I'll have a
skateboard of my own."

4

Daddy Gnu notices a bird flying overhead.

"I love birds!" he says. "That one is called a finch."

Nelly Gnu whistles at it, but she needs more practice.

"Let's whistle together," Daddy Gnu says.

Daddy Gnu and Nelly Gnu try their best birdcalls at the same time.

The finch chirps back at them!

After the bird flies away, Daddy Gnu pulls out his to-do list.

"That's a long list, Daddy," Nelly Gnu says.

Daddy Gnu agrees. But before he can get back to his chores, Daddy Gnu has to go to work at the bakery.

Nelly Gnu heads inside with Mama Gnu.

"Tomorrow is Father's Day, right, Mama?" Nelly Gnu asks. "I want to do something special to surprise Daddy, since he works so hard for all of us."

"I love that idea!" Mama Gnu replies. "Just remember, you have a playdate with Llama Llama soon."

Right on cue, the doorbell rings.

"Hi, Llama Llama!" Nelly Gnu says. She welcomes her friend inside.

Nelly Gnu explains her Father's Day plan to Llama Llama.

She wants to surprise Daddy Gnu by finishing her playhouse, since it's on his to-do list.

"That's a good idea," Llama Llama replies. "But can you *both* fit in there?"

Nelly Gnu thinks for a second.

"I guess finishing the playhouse is more a gift for me than for Daddy," Nelly Gnu says with a frown. "I have to figure out what I can do for his special Daddy's Day."

In the kitchen, Llama Llama notices Daddy Gnu's long to-do list.

"That's it!" Nelly Gnu says. "I can make Daddy a whole *new* to-do list, with only fun things on it for Father's Day!"

"That is a fantastic, one-of-a-kind idea," Mama Gnu says.

Baby Newman giggles. He agrees.

After lunch, Llama Llama helps Nelly Gnu come up with ideas for the to-do list. He suggests building something for Daddy Gnu.

"Daddy Gnu loves birds," Nelly Gnu says. "I can make him a birdhouse so birds will come visit him!"

"Daddy's car could sure use a scrub," Mama Gnu hints.

"We can wash his big red truck together," Nelly Gnu responds.

While Nelly Gnu comes up with more possibilities,

Llama Llama tries a skateboard trick of his own.

"Wow, doing an ollie is hard," he says.

That gives Nelly Gnu a great idea!

"Daddy said he'd like to have a skateboard of his own someday," Nelly Gnu remembers. "Can we get Daddy his own skateboard? It's a big present, but . . ."

"He would love that, Nelly!" Mama Gnu replies. "Let's do it!"

"Daddy says it's not a special day without a special cake," Nelly Gnu says.

Llama Llama points out that Daddy Gnu is a baker. Does that mean he'd bake his own cake?

"Maybe we can bake one for him," Nelly Gnu replies. "I'd better write all these ideas down on the fun to-do list!"

With the list finished, Mama Gnu takes Nelly Gnu and Llama Llama shopping.

They pick up supplies to make a birdhouse, ingredients to bake a cake, and a brand-new skateboard.

Nelly Gnu is ready to celebrate the best Father's Day ever!

Back home, Llama Llama helps Nelly Gnu mix the cake batter. Then they watch it rise in the oven.

Success! The cake turns out perfectly.

Once the cake is finished, it's time for Llama Llama to head home.

"Thanks for everything," Nelly Gnu says.

"I know you'll have a blast with your daddy," Llama Llama replies. "Good luck!"

The next morning, Nelly Gnu waits for her dad in the kitchen.

"I have something very important to tell you," she says. "You have a new to-do list, and we need to have this done today!"

"Better get started," Daddy Gnu replies.

Nelly Gnu jumps up from her chair.

"But wait!" she says. "This isn't a normal to-do list. It's a fun list! Happy, happy Daddy's Day!"

Outside, Daddy Gnu sees his new birdhouse for the first time. He and Nelly Gnu whistle their birdcalls together.

The finches chirp back at them from their new home!

For the next item on the fun to-do list, Nelly Gnu and her daddy wash his muddy truck.

Nelly Gnu jumps up on the hood to reach every spot.

She even draws a picture of the two of them in the soap bubbles!

Once the truck is shiny and clean, Nelly Gnu presents her daddy with the carrot cake she baked.

"Wow, someone baked *me* a cake?" Daddy Gnu asks. "What a perfect day."

But Nelly Gnu isn't finished with the to-do list just yet.

"Look, Daddy—check, check, and check," she says. "There's just one more thing . . ."

In the park, Nelly Gnu hands her daddy a present to unwrap.

"Wow, my own skateboard!" he says. "And you even put the finches on it! This is awesome."

Nelly Gnu and Daddy Gnu race down the hill together.

Mama Gnu, Newman Gnu, Llama Llama, and Mama Llama join them on their bikes and scooter!

At the bottom of the hill, Daddy Gnu gives Nelly Gnu a big hug.

"Thank you for making me feel so loved and appreciated," he says.

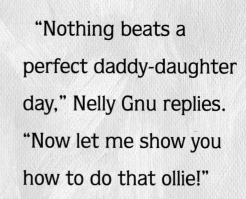

"Nothing beats a perfect daddy-daughter day," Nelly Gnu replies. "Now let me show you how to do that ollie!"